THIS CANDLEWICK BOOK BELONGS TO:

_____

_____

_____

First redesigned paperback edition 2005

The Library of Congress has cataloged the hardcover edition as follows:

Rosen, Michael, date.
This is our house / Michael Rosen ; illustrated by Bob Graham. — 1st U.S. ed.
Summary: George won't let any of the other children into his cardboard box house,
but when the tables are turned, he finds out how it feels to be excluded.
ISBN 978-1-56402-870-9 (hardcover)
[1. Selfishness—Fiction.   2. Prejudices—Fiction.   3. Sharing—Fiction.]
I. Graham, Bob, date, ill.   II. Title.
PZ7.R71867Th   1996
[E]—dc20   95-36137

ISBN 978-0-7636-0290-1 (paperback)
ISBN 978-0-7636-2816-1 (redesigned paperback)

19 20 APS 12

Printed in Humen, Dongguan, China

This book was typeset in Bob Graham font.
The illustrations were done in watercolor, ink, and colored pencil.

Candlewick Press
99 Dover Street
Somerville, Massachusetts 02144

visit us at www.candlewick.com

This Is
Our House

by
MICHAEL ROSEN

illustrated by
BOB GRAHAM

CANDLEWICK PRESS

George was in the house.

"This house is mine and no one else is coming in," George said.

"It's not your house, George," said Lindy.

"It belongs to everybody."

"No, it doesn't," said George.
"This house is all for me!"

Lindy and Marly went
for a walk over to
the swings.

"It's not George's house,
is it?" said Lindy.
"Of course it isn't," said Marly.

Lindy and Marly looked
in the window.
"It's not your house, George,
and we're coming in."

"Oh, no you're not,"
said George.
"This house isn't for girls."

Freddie was walking past with Rabbity.

"I've come to put Rabbity to bed," said Freddie.

"You can't," said George.
"This house isn't for small people like you."

Freddie took Rabbity for a ride in the car.

Charlene and Marlene fixed the front wheel.

"George won't let me and Rabbity in the house," said Freddie.

Charlene and Marlene, Freddie and Rabbity
headed straight for the house.

"Stop right there," said George.

"We're coming in to fix the fridge,"
said Charlene and Marlene.

"Oh, no you're not," said George.
"This house isn't for twins."

Luther's jumbo jet landed
in the house.
He went to get it.
"Where do you think
you're going?" said George.

"Flight 505 has crashed,"
said Luther, "and I'm
coming in for the rescue.
Fire! Fire! Wee-oo-wee-oo-
wee-oo!"

"You're not coming in here," said George.

Luther radioed for help. "Calling Dr. Sophie. Calling Dr. Sophie."

"Can I help you?" said Sophie.

"We can't get at the plane, Doctor," said Luther.

"Leave it to me," said Sophie.

Sophie and Luther pushed through the crowd.

"Make way for the doctor," said Luther.

"We're coming in," said Sophie.

"Oh, no you're not," said George. "This house isn't for people with glasses."

Rasheda had a plan. "I'm going to tunnel in."

She poked her head under the house.

"Go away," said George. "This is my house."

"Well, this is my tunnel," said Rasheda.

"Well, tunnel somewhere else," said
George. "This house isn't for
people who like tunnels."

It was getting very noisy around the house now. And hot.
And George wanted to go to the bathroom.

"I'm going to leave my house now," said George.
"AND NO ONE CAN GO IN IT WHEN I'M GONE."

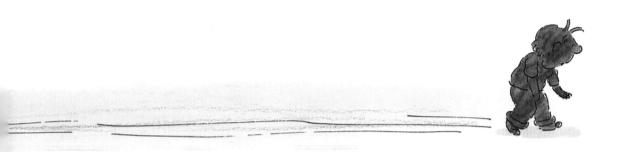

George went to the bathroom.

Lindy, Marly, Freddie, Rabbity, Marlene,
Charlene, Luther, Sophie, and Rasheda went
straight into the house.

George came back.

There was no room for George.

"This house isn't for people with red hair," said Charlene.

George started to shout.

George started to cry.

George started to stamp his
feet and kick the wall.

Then he stopped.
He looked.

"This house IS for people with red hair," said George,
". . . and for girls and small people and twins, and for
people who wear glasses and like tunnels!"

"Because . . ." shouted Lindy, Marly, Freddie,
Marlene, Charlene, Luther,
Sophie, and Rasheda,

"THIS HOUSE IS FOR EVERYONE!"

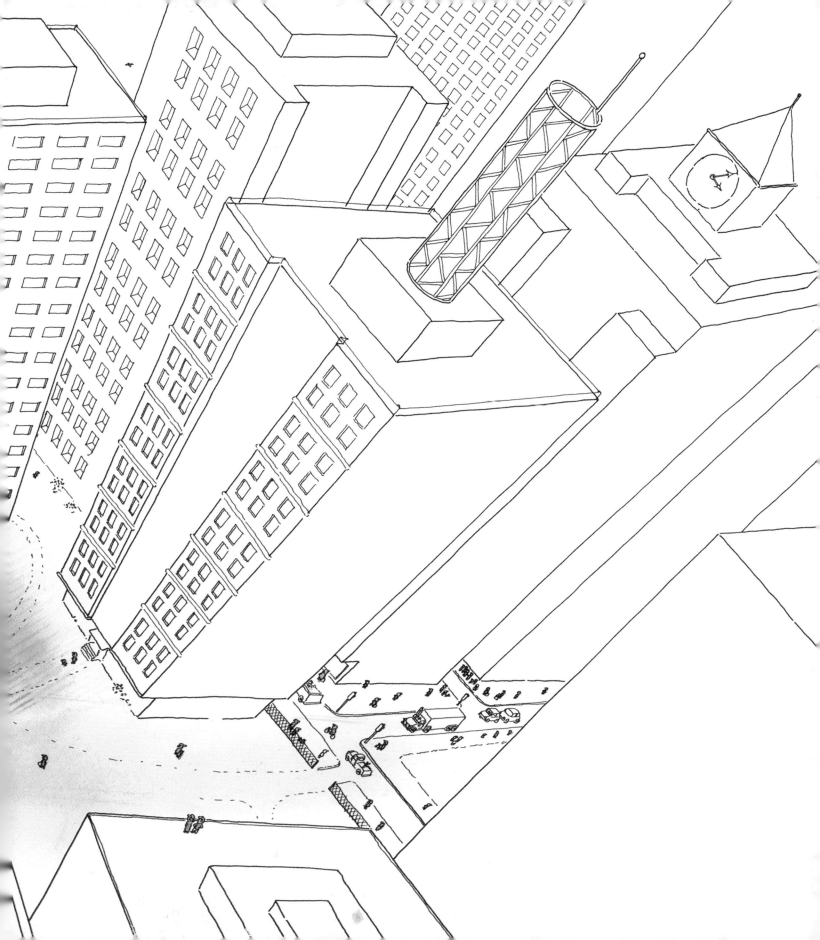

MICHAEL ROSEN observes, "Our attitudes about who's okay and who's not get formed when we're very young. I've watched how some children carve out a space for themselves using the language of discrimination. This book is a way of looking at that." A poet, storyteller, and broadcaster, Michael Rosen is also an award-winning author and anthologist of several books your young readers, including *Michael Rosen's Sad Book*, illustrated by Quentin Blake; *We're Going on a Bear Hunt*, illustrated by Helen Oxenbury; and *Shakespeare's Romeo and Juliet*, illustrated by Jane Ray.

BOB GRAHAM notes that he "used to live near several bleak public-housing buildings that surrounded a small, brightly colored playground. The playground was a suggestion of hope and, I thought, the perfect setting for this story." Bob Graham is the author-illustrator of many award-winning books for children, including *Jethro Byrd, Fairy Child*, winner of the Kate Greenaway Medal; *"Let's Get a Pup!" Said Kate*, a Boston Globe–Horn Book Award winner; *Tales from the Waterhole*; and *Oscar's Half Birthday*.